KATHY HENDERSON

Metal Muncher

Illustrated by Ant Parker

Hippo

Scholastic Children's Books,
Commonwealth House, 1-19 New Oxford Street,
London WC1A 1NU, UK
a division of Scholastic Ltd
London ~ New York ~ Toronto ~ Sydney ~ Auckland

Published in the UK by Scholastic Ltd, 1996

ISBN 0 590 13746 8

Typeset by Backup... Design and Production, London
Printed by Cox & Wyman Ltd, Reading, Berks.

10 9 8 7 6 5 4

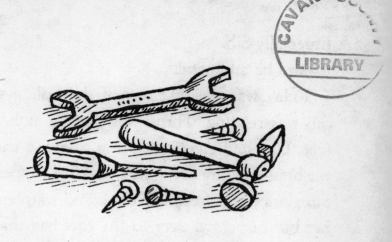

Chapter 1

The Spanner

Sibyl Thrump had a baby brother. He was round and gurgly and his name was Throgmorton but everyone called him Throg. They called her Sib. Throg was nearly one year old and he still hadn't got a tooth in his head, but he crawled like a puppy and smiled like an angel; he was always cheerful and everyone adored him.

5

Especially Sib.

And he ate metal.

Today was the first day of the holidays. Sib was reading. Throg was playing at her feet. Dad had given up trying to mend the washing-machine and was making supper. Sib glanced up from her book and watched her brother crawl over to the tool bag that was lying in the middle of the kitchen floor.

He had that twinkly, hungry look in his eye, a look she knew well. Throg reached the bag and stuck his hand into it. He took out a spanner, waved it in the air and started. First he gobbed all over it. Then he stuck it in his mouth and chomped on it. Then he sort of sucked and swallowed. And the next moment there it was. Or rather, there it wasn't.

Gone.

Throg beamed up at her and dribbled down his fat tummy. "More," he said, and stretched out his pudgy hands towards the other tools lying on the kitchen floor.

Oh, dear, thought Sib, no one's going to believe this. They never do.

Chapter 2

Ogloopa Mush

It had all started with the banana-flavoured Ogloopa Baby Mush.

"Babies love it!" proclaimed the packet.

Throg didn't.

He was four months old then and he'd never had anything except Mum's milk before. But Mum was going back to work and she said it was about time he started on "solid" food.

The face he pulled when she eased the first spoonful into his mouth would have made a statue laugh. He curled his lip and wrinkled his nose. He screwed up his eyes and stuck out his tongue. Mum and Dad and Sib all fell about laughing.

"Quick, we've got to have a picture of this," said Mum when she could breathe again. "You hold him, Sib. I'll fetch the camera."

Baby Throg sat on Sib's knee and spat Ogloopa Mush everywhere. *Pah Pah Pah!* He looked hard at the offending bowl. Then he stuck out his hand, grabbed the spoon and, carefully shaking the mush off all over the floor, he succeeded, after bumping his nose and poking his cheek, in getting the spoon into his mouth.

"Clever boy!" said Sib as he sucked contentedly. "See, it's not so bad, is it?"

"Mmm," said Throg, still sucking. The spoon seemed to get shorter. "Mmmm," he said again, pushing it in further and sucking some more. "Mmm Mmmph." And the spoon disappeared altogether.

Sib was amazed. "Mum! Dad! Throg's eaten the spoon!"

They were there in an instant. "Oh, really, Sib," said Mum anxiously. "Don't be so silly. Babies can't eat spoons."

Dad peered into Throg's toothless mouth all the same. "He couldn't swallow anything as big as a spoon. Just look. He's much too small and he hasn't any teeth to chew it up with."

"But he did, Dad. Really."

Sib's mother gave her a funny look. She looked at Dad and raised her eyebrows. Then she decided to laugh.

That evening, when Mum came to say goodnight, she sat on the edge of Sib's bed for longer than usual.

"It must be hard for you sometimes," she'd said, all sympathetic and patient, "what with the baby getting so much attention and Dad being so busy with his inventions and me going back to work next week and everything, but you must remember that we love you *very* much. So you don't need to make up any more silly stories." And she had patted Sib on the head and turned out the light.

Typical, thought Sib.

That had been eight months ago.

Chapter 3

Amazing

And it was still going on, thought Sib, as she went on reading her book. There was Throg, snacking on a spanner, and there was Dad getting the supper, his mind on other things, as if nothing had happened.

Mr Thrump carried a steaming dish of spaghetti to the table. He scooped up Throg and put him in his high chair.

"Food!" he called to Sib. "Lovely worms for tea!" Then he plonked himself down on a stool.

Sib closed her book just in time to see her father disappear under the table with a crash.

"It's *amazing*," he said as he picked himself up off the floor and inspected the buckled leg of the stool that had just collapsed under him. "Everything in this house is either old or broken or lost. Just look at this. There's a chunk out of the metal! And the door handle over there disappeared yesterday. The whole place needs sorting out. If I could only get one of my inventions selling properly and a bit of money together I'd soon get it sorted. It's just a matter of money really. That's all."

What was *really* amazing, thought Sib as she put her book down, was how for the last eight months Throg had sucked and munched and swallowed everything metal he could lay his fat little hands on but *still* neither of her parents would believe it. It wasn't just the occasional spanner or spoon, stool leg or door handle. It was every day. It was forks and knives, hinges and screws, paperclips, safety pins, saucepan lids, keys.

Sib knew. She had told them. She made sure her own bedroom door was kept shut. She hung a label on it saying "NO BABIES!" But all that got her was another lecture about how she shouldn't be jealous.

It was strange really. You wouldn't have thought either Mum or Dad were stupid. When Mum was at her job at the Building Society she handled thousands of pounds of other people's money. She ran computers. She organized things. Any money they had at home, she earned. As for Dad, Dad was an inventor. He was brilliant. He invented Bog-plugglers and Rotary-hatchits, Wheel clixers and Rod struts. He invented Pin-pullers and Pen-pushers, Plant-bottlers and Fin-openers and on top of that he looked after Sib and Throg and the house while Mum was at work.

But despite all that, neither Mum nor Dad between them seemed to have the wit to realize that they'd invented something more important than any Building Society or Rotary-hatchit, that they'd invented possibly the only metal-munching baby in the universe. That they'd invented Throg! No. Every time the cutlery disappeared or a table fell to pieces Mum just put it down to Dad being disorganized and Dad blamed lack of money.

Sib found a wooden stool and sat down at the table. Now he'd finished dusting himself off, Dad pulled up the armchair and settled cautiously in it.

"I tell you what," he said with a wide smile. "I'm going to give Mum a real surprise. Once my big meeting's over tomorrow, I'm going to get this place sorted out. Everything fixed! From top to bottom!

Just you wait."

Sib sighed and helped herself to some spaghetti. Well, you had to be kind to parents really. You couldn't expect too much.

Chapter 4

The Chance of a Lifetime

The day of Dad's big meeting had arrived at last. And where was he? At his desk? Getting ready? No. He was under the sink with his bottom sticking out.

Today he had been asked to bring the designs for his Multi-Phasing Swivvit-Groveller to show to Mr Oshi, the Research Director of the mighty Mitzimasha Manufacturing Company. It was the chance of a lifetime.

"They're the biggest manufacturers in the world. It's a real honour. They never ask twice," said Dad over breakfast.

"If they take it on, we could be rich!" he had said to Mum as she rushed out of the door, late for work as usual.

"We'll be able to do what we want!" he shouted after her as she tore up the street.

"And as for National Gadgets Inc.," he said to Throg, who was sitting on his hip, "we'll show them, Throggety-Pog. We'll show them!" and he did a little dance on the doorstep.

The National Gadget Company Incorporated was Mr Thrump's pet hate. Its products were faulty. Its machines fell apart. Worse still, he knew they were crooks but he couldn't prove it. Oh, yes, they'd shown interest in his designs. They'd looked at them a number of times. But they never actually bought any of them. Instead, by some mysterious coincidence, National Gadgets always seemed to bring out their

26

own half-baked second-rate version of his inventions just after he'd finished inventing them. Mr Thrump knew they were stealing his ideas but he couldn't work out how. Still, today he didn't care. Mitzimasha Manufacturing was worth ten National Gadget Companies.

"Mitzimasha here we come," he sang happily as he cleared the breakfast, "National Gadgets up your bum."

In fact he felt so cheerful that he not only emptied the rubbish bin, he even swept out the cupboard under the sink where the bin was kept. That was when he discovered the leaky pipe.

"Well, there's no time like the present," he whistled. "I said I'd start today and a pipe like that won't take a minute to fix!" That was why he was under the sink now.

"Pass me the spanner, Sib," came his muffled voice.

"I can't, Dad."

Throg clapped his hands. "More?" he beamed.

"Oh, go on Sib! I don't want to let go of this joint in case it bursts."

"But I *can't*, Dad."

"Why ever not?"

"I told you. Throg ate it yesterday."

Dad backed out of the cupboard and banged his head. *Thump* it went. He scowled and started to search through the tool bag. *Clank. Clunk.* Throg looked interested. "More?" he beamed cheerfully. Dad chucked him under the chin and smiled. Then he turned to Sib.

"You know something, Sibyl Thrump," he said sternly, "I've had just about enough of this nonsense. Your brother is a BABY. He is not a monster or a metal detector or a garbage disposal unit." *Clink*. "And the sooner you get used to the idea and stop blaming him for every little problem that crops up, the BETTER!" *Clump*. "I know that blasted spanner is here somewhere," he muttered, lifting the bag off the floor to peer underneath it and then dropping it heavily again.

The floor shook. Across the room there was a muffled *thud*. With a *hissssss!* and a *whoooooosh!* water started squirting out from under the sink at a million miles a minute.

Can YOU read four Young Hippo books?

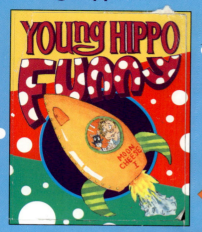

YOUNG HIPPO Readometer

The Young Hippo is sending a special prize to everyone who collects any four of these stickers, which can be found in Young Hippo books.

This is one sticker to stick on your own Young Hippo Readometer Card!

Collect four stickers and fill up your Readometer Card

There are all these stickers to collect too!

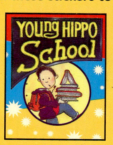

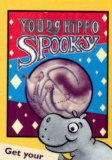

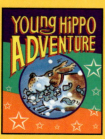

Get your Young Hippo Readometer Card from your local bookshop, or by sending your name and address to:

Young Hippo Readometer Card Requests, Scholastic Children's Books, 6th Floor, Commonwealth House, 1-19 New Oxford Street, London WC1A 1NU

Offer begins March 1997

Chapter 5

Mitzimasha Here I Come

It took them the rest of morning to clear up. Dad fixed. Sib mopped. Throg watched and smiled and gurgled and sang. Then he got hungry, sucked a lump out of the side of the bucket and fell asleep in the armchair. By the time they'd finished and had some lunch it was nearly time for Dad to leave.

"Mitzimasha here I come," he sang. Then

33

he caught sight of himself in the mirror. His trousers were soaking wet. His hair was standing on end and there was baby food all down his front where Throg had spat his lunch at him. "Oh, no," he said. "Just look at me, Sib. I can't go like this!" And off he went to change.

Sib settled down to finish her book. She'd only read half a chapter when Dad was back.

"Look at the time!" he fretted. "I don't know where your mum is but I'll have to go in a minute … just as soon as I've got the designs out. Well? How do I look, Sib?"

Dad had put on a clean jacket and some trousers that almost matched. His shirt had most of its buttons and looked as if it might have been ironed once. He was wearing a tie and polished shoes. He'd even squashed his hair down.

"Brilliant, Dad," said Sib. "You look really smart."

Dad was struggling to fasten his belt. Then he stopped. With a puzzled look on his face he pulled the long leather strap out of the loops at the top of his trousers.

"How on earth can a buckle disappear from a belt?" he said.

Throg hiccupped in his sleep.

Mr Thrump found a piece of string to tie his trousers up with and went down to the cellar to get the plans for the Swivvit-Groveller out of his top-security store.

Throg snoozed. Sib finished *Bog Weevil* and started on *Earth Skimmer*. She was just taking off into the outer planisphere when the phone rang. It was Mum. She sounded urgent.

"Tell Dad that I'm on my way but I've been held up at work. I'm going to be late. If he needs to leave before I get there, you and Throg go and wait next door with Mrs Shiner. I'll pick you up when I get back. All right? Bye."

The phone had woken Throg. He sat up and wailed.

"Come on," said Sib, picking him up and cuddling him. "Let's go and give Dad the message."

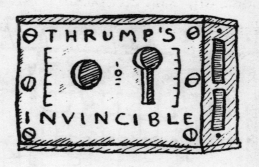

Chapter 6

The Cage

Mr Thrump kept the plans and models of his new inventions in a sort of huge walk-in cupboard in the cellar. He called it "The Cage". It had brick walls and a stout wooden door on the outside. Inside there was a second layer of strong steel mesh and a steel mesh door fastened with a "Thrump's Invincible" lock – *"unpickable, uncrackable,*

can't be blown up or sawn through". With the National Gadget Company on the prowl Dad wasn't taking any chances.

Sib was halfway down the cellar stairs with Throg when she heard a strange clicking sound. She looked round. At the far end of the cellar, behind the cage, where it was usually pitch dark, there seemed to be a faint grey light. It was coming from the street side of the house.

"Mitzimasha, what a smasher," sang Dad cheerfully inside the open cage. Throg grizzled. Riding him in her arms, Sib walked round behind the cage to find out where the light was coming from.

That was odd. Where the cellar ran underneath the pavement, the lid of the old coal delivery hole was off and daylight was trickling down from the street. Odder still was the unmistakable shape of a camera

sticking nose-first into the back wall of the cage and clicking away. What on earth, thought Sib, would anyone want with a camera sticking into Dad's top-security store?

Before she could even finish the thought someone had grabbed her from behind and with one black-gloved hand over her mouth was pushing her and Throg firmly back towards the open door of the cage.

"That you, Sib?" said Dad, not turning round.

There was a clang and a bang and the decisive click of the key being turned in the Thrump's Invincible lock. Sib found herself and Throg firmly locked inside the cage with her astonished father.

A mocking voice came from round the corner. "Mitzimasha indeed! We can't have that, Mr Thrump. You're much too useful. Somehow I don't think you're going to be keeping your appointment today. And you know what they say: 'No second chances with Mitzimasha'. Ha ha ha ha." The laughing voice got further away. "On behalf of National Gadgets, may I wish you a comfortable afternoon!"

There was a clunk as the coal-hole cover was pushed back into place from outside.

Throg wailed.

Dad's mouth opened and shut, opened and shut.

Finally he got some words out. "I've *got* to get out of here," he said. "I've *got* to get to that appointment!"

Chapter 7

Thrump's Invincible

Sib rattled at the steel mesh door.

"That won't do any good," said Dad miserably.

"*Waaaaaah!*" went Throg.

"What about the key?" asked Sib.

"They've taken it."

"*Waaaaaaah!*"

"Haven't you got another?"

"Yes, but it's upstairs."

"What about a saw or a tool?"

"They're all in the workshop. Besides, they wouldn't do any good. That lock's a Thrump's Invincible."

"*Waaaaaaaaaaaaaaaaaaaaaah!*"

"No, our only hope is that Mum gets back soon."

Suddenly Sib remembered the telephone message. Her heart sank. "She rang, Dad.

She got held up. She's going to be late."

It was the last straw.

"The creeps!" shouted Mr Thrump. "The stinkbags! The dirty rotten thieving cheating snot-faced double-crossing CROOKS!"

Throg was so astonished that he stopped wailing and sucked his fingers hungrily instead. There was silence.

Dad subsided like a punctured balloon. He buried his face in his hands. His voice was quiet now. "That's it, then. I've missed my chance. My one big chance."

Throg leaned over and patted Dad's head with his gobby fingers. "More. More," he said sympathetically.

"There is one thing, Dad," said Sib.

"Hmm." Dad did not sound hopeful.

"Promise you won't tell me off?"

"Hmm."

"No, I mean *really* promise. No lectures? Not a single word?"

Dad looked up, dead serious. "If it'll get me out of here in time I'll promise anything."

"Well there is…" Sib hesitated to say it. She had to admit it sounded weird. And she didn't want to strain Dad's brain too much. He was upset enough already. "There is … er…"

"What is there?"

"There's Throg."

"Throg?"

"Yes, Throg… You see, like I've been trying to tell you… Throg … eats … metal."

Dad went red in the face and started to splutter.

"Dad. Dad. You promised, Dad!" Sib pleaded.

With difficulty, he stopped himself from saying anything. Instead he buried his face in his hands again. Sib took this as agreement.

"Come on, Throg," she said, moving him on to her other hip and squeezing up to the door.

Throg looked puzzled.

"Look." Sib stuck out her tongue and licked gingerly at one of the bars. It tasted revolting. Throg understood at once. He was the expert after all. He was also very hungry.

Fastening his toothless gums round the top of the Thrump's Invincible he began to slobber and suck. *Chomp chomp* went Throg, *chomp slick chomp*. And there in the cellar Throgmorton Thrump sucked and sucked until every last trace of the Thrump's Invincible had completely disappeared.

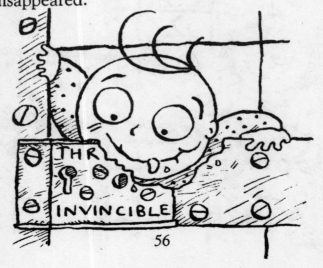

Dad looked up, stunned, as the door swung harmlessly open. "Go on!" said Sib, thrusting the designs into his hand. "If you hurry you can still make it."

Chapter 8

Perhaps....?

He did. He made it! He got there!

One bicycle, two trains and a taxi later, Mr Thrump raced up the stairs of the famous Mitzimasha Building two at a time with his tie flapping and his hair flying and arrived gasping on the twenty-sixth floor with exactly three seconds to spare.

Mr Fitzwilliam Oshi, Research Director

of the Mitzimasha Manufacturing Company, was very courteous. Ignoring the sweat running down Dad's face, he shook his hand, invited him into his office and offered him a cup of tea.

Mr Oshi examined the designs for the Swivvit-Groveller with interest. He asked sensible questions. He made suggestions for improvements. He talked Grommit-Thwackers and Waffledroppers and, exactly

twenty minutes after the start of the meeting, he offered Dad some money to develop his idea further and to produce a full-size working model to bring back in six months' time.

"Then we can talk contracts!" smiled Mr Oshi, bowing goodbye.

Dad glided down the twenty-six floors of the Mitzimasha Building as if he was in a dream, not a lift. He floated out through the great glass doors on to the street and only came back to earth when a passing bus nearly chopped his toes off. Stepping back

on to the pavement he shook himself, and
then, to the amazement of the staring bus
passengers, he jumped into the air and
yelled, "Yippee!"

It was too much for the string round his
waist. It snapped with the shock and his
trousers tumbled down round his ankles.

Sib and Throg waited at Mrs Shiner's. Sib had some cake. Throg wasn't hungry.

"Bless his little heart," said Mrs Shiner. "Isn't he well?" But Sib knew that there was no point trying to explain.

When Mum got back she was all apologies. "I'm so sorry, Mrs Shiner. Sorry, Sib. There was nothing I could do."

"Mum," said Sib, "you're not going to believe what's been going on!"

How right she was.

Later, when the excitement had died down and Throg had gone to sleep, Sib heard her parents talking in the other room.

"About Throg..." she heard Dad say. "Do you think Sib might have a point?"

"How do you mean?"

"Well, that he might be sort of... Different... Unusual...?" He seemed to be having difficulty finding the right words.

"…Special or something?"

"Special?" said Mum. "*Of course* he's special. *Both* the children are special."

"I mean, what Sib says…" Dad took a deep breath. "About him eating metal…"

Mum was tired. "Oh, no," she snapped. "Don't you start! I've had quite enough trouble with Sib today already! Metal eating indeed! Of course the children are special, but you don't seriously expect me to believe that they've got superhuman powers do you? The truth is that you got into one of your muddles and they got you out of it. That's all. There's bound to be a perfectly good explanation."

Dad wasn't listening. "I'd never have got out of the cage in time without their help," he mused. "And as for that lock... I've never seen anything like it... I can't understand what happened to it at all."

Sib stared across at Throg in his cot. His eyes were closed. His hair was downy and he was sucking his thumb and snuffling in his sleep just like any ordinary baby. She closed her book. It wasn't as interesting as Throg anyway. But then you couldn't put someone as interesting as Throg in a book because nobody would believe the story.

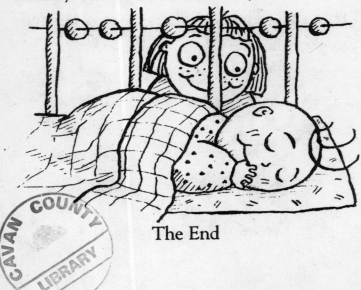

The End

Five *more* Young Hippo Funnies to make you laugh!

Bod's Mum's Knickers
Peter Beere

Count Draco Down Under
Ann Jungman

Emily H and the Enormous Tarantula

Emily H and the Stranger in the Castle

Emily H Turns Detective
Kara May

Or dare you try a Young Hippo Spooky?

Ghost Dog
Eleanor Allen

The Screaming Demon Ghostie
Jean Chapman

The Green Hand
Tessa Krailing

Smoke Cat
Linda Newbery

The Kings' Castle
Mr Wellington Boots
Ann Ruffell

Scarem's House
Malcolm Yorke

Class No. _____J_____ Acc No. C93763

Author: HENDERSON, K Loc: / / AUG 2000

LEABHARLANN
CHONDAE AN CHABHAIN

_____

_____

_____

1. **This book may be kept three weeks. It is to be returned on / before the last date stamped below.**
2. **A fine of 20p will be charged for every week or part of week a book is overdue.**

	/ / JAN 2003	